FOLLOW THE TRAIL,
DIGSBY THE MOLE

For Jill and Chris

First published in Great Britain in 1996 by Sapling, an imprint of
Boxtree Limited, Broadwall House, 21 Broadwall, London SE1 9PL.

10 9 8 7 6 5 4 3 2 1

ISBN: 0 7522 0612 5

Origination by Loudwater
Printed and bound in Italy by L.E.G.O

A CIP catalogue entry is available from the British Library.

FOLLOW THE TRAIL, DIGSBY THE MOLE

KATE VEALE

Be careful not to get stuck in this pipe

Digsby is an inquisitive mole - he can't resist climbing into anything that looks interesting, especially old pipes and drains, tunnels and holes. His favourite saying is "I'll look into it!" And that is exactly what he does . . .

IMPORTANT NOTICE

PLEASE DO NOT LOOK

INSIDE THIS PIPE

One day, Digsby was walking along the street wearing his everyday waistcoat, when he came across a dustbin with the lid half off. He hesitated "I'll look into it," he decided. So, with great difficulty, he climbed up the side to peer in. CLANG! He overbalanced and crashed head first into the bin.

"What shall I do now?" he wailed.
He was stuck in the rubbish at
the bottom of the dustbin with a
small plastic tub wedged on his
head like a helmet.
Suddenly he heard voices and
a great deal of banging. Then
he felt the dustbin being lifted
high up into the air.

"Help!" shouted Digsby
as he shot out of the bin. But there
was too much noise for anyone to hear,
and he was carried away in the dustcart
to the big dump and tipped out again.

There he was, deep in the middle of the dump
with a lot of rubbish on top of him.
"How will I ever find my way out of this?"
cried Digsby.
To his great surprise a voice
answered: "Follow my trail
and you will find your
way home."

Digsby tried to pull the plastic tub off his head so that he could hear better. The voice seemed to be coming from above him.

"You can't see me at the moment," said the voice. "I'm sitting on top of the plastic tub on your head."

"Who are you?" asked Digsby.

"I'm the Head of the Highways for the dump," said the voice, "and my name is Jelly."

Jelly slid down, leaving a thin silvery trail behind him, and sat on an empty matchbox in front of Digsby.

Digsby peered out from under his plastic helmet. He could dimly see that Jelly was a big orange slug.

"If you don't follow my trail you will never find
your way out, ever," warned Jelly seriously. "It is
very important. Don't listen to anyone else; just
follow my silvery trail and you'll be all right."
Jelly slid into the matchbox. "The trail starts
here, and will lead you to the edge of the dump.
You'll find your way home from there. I'm going
to sleep now. Good luck!"
With that, Jelly curled up.

FOLLOW THE SILVERY TRAIL

THIS WAY ⇨

Digsby thanked Jelly and set off with the plastic tub still stuck on his head. He climbed up through the pile of rubbish taking great care to follow the silvery trail. It went through old buckets, over cans and dented saucepans.

THIS WAY

The trail went through piles of grass cuttings, over squeezy bottles and into heaps of vegetable peelings. Digsby met a shiny blue beetle eating the peelings.
"I know a much better way out of the dump if you would like to follow me," said the blue beetle.
"Thank you very much, but I'm following Jelly the slug's silvery trail," said Digsby. And carried on his way.
The trail went across the spokes of a rusty bike wheel and through an old yoghurt pot which Digsby got stuck in.

THIS WAY ⇨

FULL FAT YOGHURT

He got a plastic
tube stuck on his arm.
Then Digsby came across
a centipede in an old boot.
"Would you like to come
this way? I know a good
way out of the dump," it said.
"No, thank you," replied Digsby.
"I'm following the silvery trail.

He met a cheeky rat. "Nice suit," laughed the rat. Digsby ignored him and struggled on. He must be nearly out of the dump by now. He felt something sticky spilling over him and then a bag of flour split open and covered him.

At last he climbed out in to the
clean air. Digsby was so glad to be
out of the dump that he ran as fast as he
could in the yoghurt pot with the plastic helmet
on his head, aross the fields towards home. The
first house he came to was Oliver Otter's.

"What's happened to you?" asked Oliver.
"You look as if you've seen a ghost and why
are you wearing a yoghurt pot and a helmet?"
"It's a long story," sighed Digsby.
Oliver cut him out of the
yoghurt pot and the
plastic helmet and
Digsby had a bath.

When he was nice and clean he came back into the kitchen to join Oliver.

Oliver was finishing his dinner.

"I'm just having some orange jelly for pudding," Oliver said. "Would you like some, too?"

"No thank you, Oliver," gulped Digsby. "I don't think I could face eating any jelly tonight."

In fact, Digsby has been unable to eat any sort of jelly for a long time now . . .

and he hasn't looked in any dustbins either!

THE END